ART
LESSONS

By Eleanor Schick

Greenwillow Books, New York

07

**For Ou Mie Shu,
because he is an artist**

Library of Congress Cataloging-in-Publication Data
Schick, Eleanor (date)
Art lessons.
Summary: A young student learns about art and
life from his special friend and art teacher.
[1. Art — Fiction.   2. Teachers — Fiction.
3. Friendship — Fiction]   I. Title.
PZ7.S3445Ar   1987   [E]   86-243
ISBN 0-688-05120-0
ISBN 0-688-05121-9 (lib. bdg.)

Contents

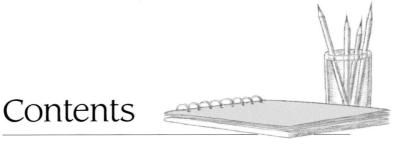

4

ADRIANNE

Adrianne is an artist. She lives next door to us. Her garage is where she paints and draws. That is why she calls it her studio. In summer, when it is hot, Adrianne works outside.

Adrianne has been working late tonight. I have been resting on the cool grass.

Adrianne comes out, closing her
studio. The moon is coming up
behind the mountains. Adrianne
stands, watching it. We both watch
the moon.

Adrianne sits on the grass with
me. We talk about the smells of
summer in the air. The moon's
color changes from yellow to white
as it rises in the sky. Adrianne tells
me she is painting the moon and
the mountains in her mind, as she
watches them.

I tell Adrianne I love to draw. She asks to see my drawings. I bring her the ones I keep in my dresser drawer. She looks at each one for a long time, sometimes smiling, sometimes very serious. She gives them back to me.

"I will be your teacher, if you like,"
Adrianne says. "No money. Just because
we're friends. You can come and draw
with me sometimes."

ADRIANNE'S STUDIO

Now I go to Adrianne's studio, to draw with her.

Today she has set out a single red
flower in a glass vase, on a yellow
mat.

We draw together. We draw the
flower, and the vase, and the mat.

We talk very little. We only look, and draw, look and draw.

"I like to do this," I tell Adrianne. "It feels peaceful."

Adrianne says, "Drawing is meditation. Just do it, and peace comes."

AT THE ZOO

One day Adrianne takes me to the zoo, to draw the tigers. We stop at their cage. They are sleeping in the sun.

Adrianne sits very still. She looks
around, studying.

I draw the tigers. I am excited, just
to be near them.

Adrianne draws flowers.

Before we go home, I show
Adrianne my tiger drawings.
"They are very strong," she says.
She shows me her flowers. They
are bright with pinks and oranges,
yellows and reds.

I say to myself, "Next time I will draw flowers, too." But when we return to the zoo, the flowers are not in bloom anymore. Now I understand why Adrianne didn't draw tigers last time.

AT THE RIVER

Adrianne and I walk to the river
one hot summer evening.
"This time we wait, before we draw,"
she says to me.

Adrianne and I stand very still,
watching the river. She points out
how the water makes a mirror
picture of the houses and trees
on the opposite shore.

The picture is rippled, like the
water, and it is upside down.

"An artist must learn to look before
he draws," Adrianne says.

After I look for a long time, I see much more. When I draw, I put the trees high up on my paper, so I have room for the mirror picture in the water below them.

AT THE PARK

One afternoon Adrianne knocks at my door to remind me we are going drawing.

"I'm sad," I tell her. "I don't want to talk about it, but I'm sad today, and I don't want to draw."

Adrianne says, "An artist draws in sadness and in joy. Whatever happens, he never stops drawing."

I go with Adrianne to the park.
We draw the trees and the sky,
the people and the kites, and the
birds. I work on one drawing all
afternoon. It's the most special
drawing I've ever done.

I name it, "Sad Day at the Park."
Adrianne thinks it's special, too.

AT THE MUSEUM

Adrianne says, "You are ready to see the art in the museum." We go together.

In one room an art student is
copying a painting.

"You're not supposed to copy,"
  I tell Adrianne.
"Not supposed to copy in order
  to cheat or pretend," Adrianne
  says, "but to learn, yes."
"I don't understand," I say.
"The way to learn is to study,"
  Adrianne explains.
"One way to study is to copy."

When I get home, I take an art
book down from the shelf.

I copy one of the drawings. I work
so hard, I forget to be hungry.
Mom has to call me three times for
dinner. After dinner I finish my
drawing. I like what I have done.
I will show it to Adrianne, and
she will see that I am learning.

NAPKIN PICTURES

One day I meet Adrianne at the soda shop. We buy ice cream cones, and sit down at a table.

We talk, and laugh, and eat ice
cream together.

Adrianne takes a napkin and draws
a picture of me.

I take a napkin and draw a picture
of her.

"An artist has to be clever," says
Adrianne. "When there's no paper,
he uses whatever he can find. The
important thing is never to miss a
good picture." She gives me the
drawing she has made. When I
bring it home, Mom says, "We'll
frame it. The soft design of the
napkin makes it even more
beautiful."

Now Adrianne's napkin drawing

hangs in a frame, on my wall.

THE FAIR

At the end of summer, I go with
Adrianne to the arts-and-crafts
fair in the park. We see paintings
and jewelry, hand sewn blouses,
wood carvings, and quilts.

Adrianne talks to the people about
the things they have made.
"It doesn't matter whether they are
great works of art or not," she says
to me. "What matters is that they
were made with love."

Adrianne says, "People think art is a mystery. They want to know the secret. Some say the secret is love. Some say hard work. I say both are true.

"Still, the artist must never forget,
his painting of a bird may be called
great, but the bird itself is greater.

"How beautiful it all is," Adrianne
says. "Drawing helps us to see it."
We walk through the park for a
long time before we go home.